This book belongs to
_____

This book is dedicated to my children - Mikey, Kobe, and Jojo.

Copyright © 2024 Grow Grit Press LLC. All rights reserved. No part of this book may be reproduced in any form without permission in writing from the publisher. Please send bulk order requests to info@ninjalifehacks.tv

Paperback ISBN: 978-1-63731-888-1
Hardcover ISBN: 978-1-63731-890-4
eBook ISBN: 978-1-63731-889-8

Printed and bound in the USA.
NinjaLifeHacks.tv

Ninja Life Hacks®
by Mary Nhin

Loyal Ninja

A Book About the Importance of Loyalty

Ninja Life Hacks®
by Mary Nhin

If I made a promise, I had a hard time keeping my word.

When my team was losing, I quickly traded teams.

It wasn't until Authentic Ninja shared with me the ninja life hack of L.O.Y.A.L. that I learned the true meaning of loyalty!

O is for **Offer help**. Being loyal means offering a helping hand whenever a friend is in need. It's like being a superhero with a cape made of kindness!

I spotted Angry Ninja struggling with his kite tangled in a tree. Without hesitation, I rushed over to offer my help. Together, we untangled the kite and sent it soaring into the sky!

Y is for **Your word**. To be loyal, you want to keep your promises and be someone your friends can trust. It's like planting seeds of friendship that bloom into beautiful flowers!

When I promised to meet Brave Ninja at the playground, I made sure to keep my word, even though it started raining. I didn't want to let her down, so I dashed through the puddles to meet her.

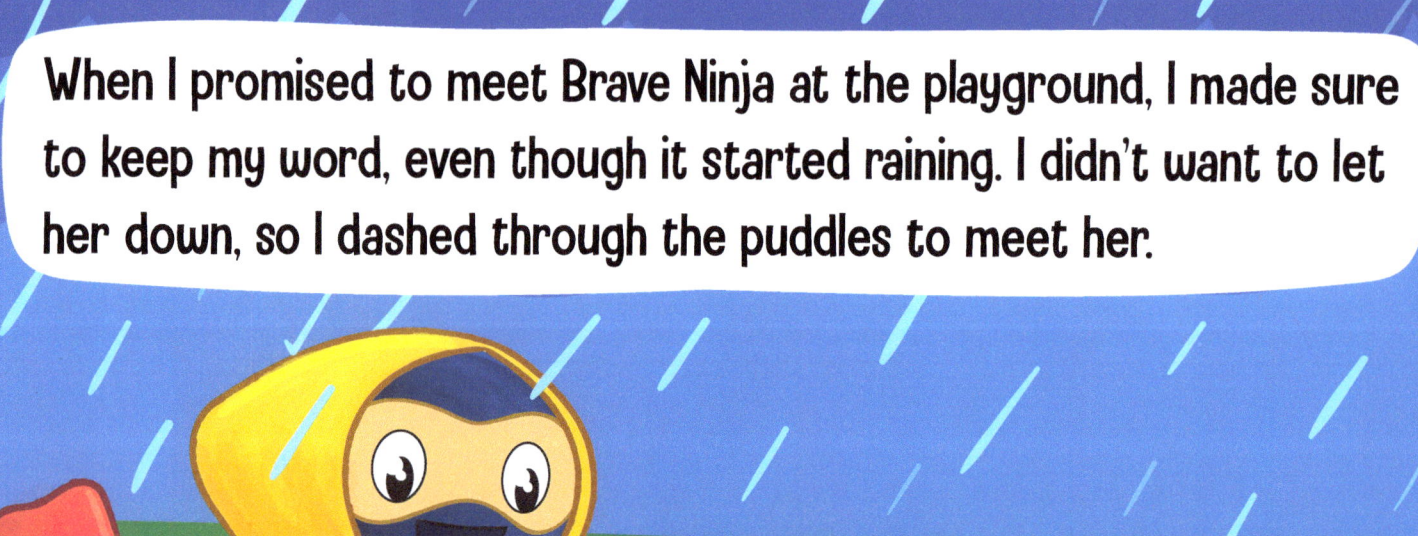

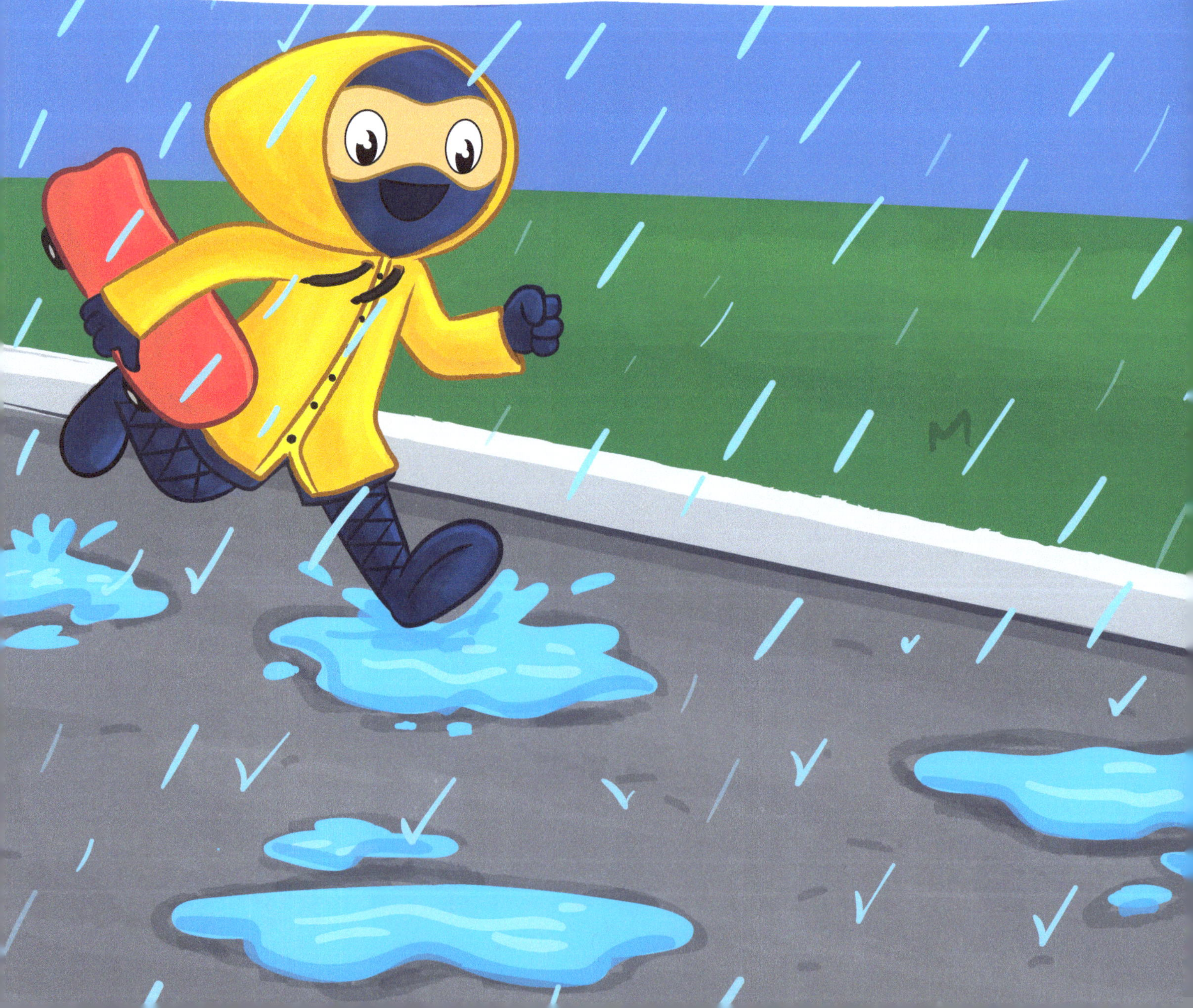

A is for **Always be There**. Being loyal means standing by your friends through thick and thin, like an umbrella that shields them from the wind and rain.

L is for **Love**. To be loyal, you can show love and kindness to everyone around you. It's like sprinkling glitter of happiness wherever I go!

As I continued along the path, I picked flowers for my mom and shared my snacks with the birds in the park. It made my heart feel warm and fuzzy to spread love and joy to others.

From that day on, I made a promise to always **listen**, **offer help**, keep **your word**, **always be there**, and spread **love** wherever I go. And you know what? You can be a loyal friend too!

Remembering the magic of L.O.Y.A.L. could be your secret weapon in developing loyalty!

www.ingramcontent.com/pod-product-compliance
Lightning Source LLC
Chambersburg PA
CBHW041522070526
44585CB00002B/41